Green Kids

Saving Water

Neil Morris

QEB Publishing

Published in the United States by
QEB Publishing, Inc.
3 Wrigley, Suite A
Irvine, CA 92618

www.qeb-publishing.com

Library of Congress Control Number: 2008010280

ISBN 978 1 59566 542 3

Printed and bound in United States

Author Neil Morris
Consultant Bibi van der Zee
Editor Amanda Askew
Designer Elaine Wilkinson
Picture Researcher Maria Joannou
Illustrator Mark Turner for Beehive Illustration

Publisher Steve Evans
Creative Director Zeta Davies

Picture credits (fc = front cover, t = top, b = bottom,
l = left, r = right)

Corbis Ashley Cooper 7t, Envision 9,
Estelle Klawitter/ Zefa 13, H Schmid/ Zefa 15,
Mark Bolton 16–17, Richard Smith 21

Dreamstime 8, 19

Getty Images Taxi/ James Ross 17

Istockphoto 20

Shutterstock Thomas M Perkins 2, Andi Berger 4,
Denise Kappa 5, Katrina Brown 7b, 10r, 10l, 12,
Lisa F Young 14, Dejan Lazarevic 18,
Andrey Armyagov fc

Words in **bold** can be
found in the glossary
on page 22.

Contents

Water everywhere   4

Where does water come from?   6

Drinking water   8

All sorts of uses   10

Turn off the faucet!   12

Drip, drip, drip   14

Collecting and recycling   16

Dirty water   18

Around the world   20

Glossary   22

Index   23

Notes for parents and teachers   24

Water everywhere

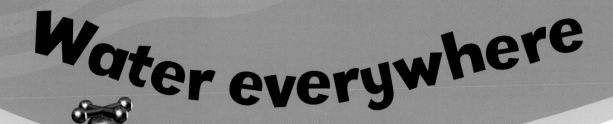

Water is all around us. It covers nearly three-quarters of our planet. The world's oceans, lakes, and rivers are full of water. A lot of it is salty, which means we cannot drink it.

Did you know?

Water is inside every one of us, as well as all around us. Two-thirds of our body is made of water— including the brain, muscles, skin, and blood.

All living things need water to live. We must drink lots of **fresh water** every day to stay healthy. Water is very valuable to us. It is important to use it wisely and save as much as we can.

▲ A lot of water can be saved if you water plants using a watering can, rather than a garden hose.

Where does water come from?

Water comes from rain and it moves in a never-ending cycle. The water cycle is the journey water takes when it leaves the Earth's surface, goes into the sky, and then returns to the Earth's surface.

The Water Cycle

1. Rain falls from clouds in the sky.
2. It flows to the sea in streams and rivers.
3. Heat from the Sun changes some of the liquid water into a gas called water vapor. The water vapor rises and makes more clouds.
4. Then the cycle starts again.

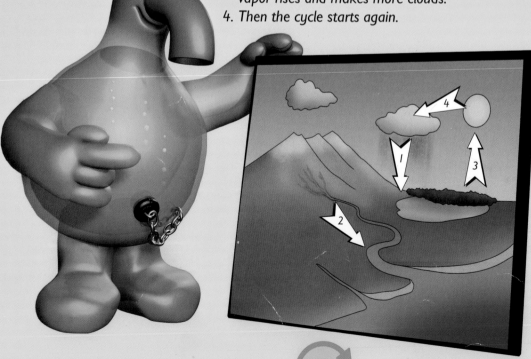

Fresh water is pumped to our homes, schools, offices, and stores through large underground pipes. We just have to turn on the faucet to get water!

▲ *Large water pipes called* **mains** *are laid and buried underground.*

You can do it

You can see how much rain falls by leaving an empty pot, such as a glass jar, outside. Mark on the glass how much rain falls each day, and keep a weekly rain diary.

Friday

Wednesday

Tuesday

Monday

Drinking water

Some people get water from **springs** and **wells**. Drinking water comes from **reservoirs**. To make it safe to drink, the water is cleaned at a treatment works.

▲ Water is cleaned in these tanks at a treatment works.

Did you know?

It is impossible to think of a drink without water! Tea and coffee are made with hot water. There is water in fruit juices and sodas, too.

Some people buy sparkling or still water in bottles. If clean water is available from a faucet, then bottled water is a waste of energy. This is because it takes extra energy to make the bottles and fill, label, and transport them to stores.

▼ Supermarkets sell many different brands of bottled water, from different springs around the world.

All sorts of uses

▲ We need water to clean dirty dishes. We can save water by not letting the faucet run.

Water is also used for washing, cooking, cleaning clothes, and flushing the toilet. This adds up to an enormous amount of water, so we should only use as much as we need.

Some people use huge amounts of water without thinking. A garden sprinkler, for example, can use 160 gallons (600 liters) of water in an hour. That is a bathful every eight minutes!

You can do it

How much water does your family use?

• Washing machine load–130 pints (60 liters) • Bath–170 pints (80 liters)
• Shower–65 pints (30 liters)
• Toilet flush–20 pints (10 liters)

Turn off the faucet!

Lots of clean water is wasted down the plughole of the bathroom or kitchen sink. The water flows through drains into large underground pipes, called **sewers**.

▲ This waste water is flowing straight back into a river.

There is an easy way to save water. When you are washing things, do not let the water run any longer than it has to. Use just the water you need and then turn off the faucet.

You can do it

Just for once, leave the cold faucet running when you brush your teeth. If you leave the plug in, you can see how much water you've wasted. You'll be amazed!

Drip, drip, drip

Water is also wasted if faucets do not work properly. A dripping faucet might seem unimportant, but it could waste more than 50 pints (25 liters) of water a day.

▲ *A plumber fixes water pipes if they have a leak.*

Did you know?

Water companies repair pipes all the time, but there are still big leaks. Most companies lose at least one-tenth of their water through broken pipes.

Many modern washing machines and dishwashers use less water than older models.

They also save energy. We can save even more by only running them when they are full.

▲ A washing machine that is only half full wastes water and energy.

Collecting and recycling

We can reuse water on plants in the garden. The waste water left after washing vegetables or water from showers, kitchen sinks, and washing machines is called "gray water." It is not drinkable, but it can be reused.

Rainwater can be collected and used to water plants. The easiest way is to use a barrel called a water butt. It gathers water from a drainpipe.

Did you know?

If you clean the family car with water in buckets, you might use 65 pints (30 liters). Using a hosepipe would use six times as much!

◀ A water butt can store water during winter when it rains a lot. This can then be used in summer to water plants when there is little rain.

Dirty water

Some farmers spray **chemicals** on their crops to help them to grow and to protect them from pests. These chemicals can **pollute** underground water and nearby water sources, such as rivers.

Did you know?

More than one billion people in the world live without clean water-that's one in every six people.

Factories produce chemicals that can pollute rivers. Waste gases from cars and factories are also a problem. They mix with water in clouds to make **acid rain**. When acid rain falls, it can pollute lakes, kill trees, and harm wildlife.

▼ *These trees have been damaged by acid rain.*

Around the world

In rich countries of the world, most people use about 50 gallons (200 liters) of clean water each day. In poorer regions, water is much more precious—people only have 30 pints (15 liters) each.

▲ A reservoir is a large store of clean, fresh water.

You can do it

Make a poster to help people understand why it is important to save water and what they can do to help.

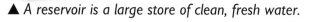

▲ Some villages do not have clean running water, so people walk many miles to find water.

In parts of Africa, there is often very little rainfall. This can cause a **drought** and the ground dries up. People get clean drinking water from a well. Dirty drinking water can make people very ill.

Glossary

acid rain   rain that has been polluted by waste gases

chemical   a substance made by mixing other substances together

drought   a period of very dry weather with no rainfall. The ground dries up

fresh water   water that is not salty so we can drink it

mains   underground pipes used to send water to buildings

pollute   to damage the environment with harmful substances

reservoir   a lake where water is stored

sewer   a large underground pipe that carries dirty water away

spring   a place where water flows naturally out of the ground

well   a hole dug to get underground water

Index

acid rain 19

bath 11

cars 17, 19
clouds 6, 19

drains 12
drinking water
5, 8, 9, 21
drought 21

factories 19
faucets 7, 10, 12,
14
fresh water 7, 20

gray water 16

lakes 4, 19

pipes 7, 12, 14
pollution 18, 19

rain 6, 7, 16, 17
reservoirs 8, 20
rivers 4, 6, 12,
18, 19

salty water 4
shower 11
springs 8, 9

toilet 10, 11

washing 10, 12
washing machine
11, 15
water butt 16, 17
water cycle 6
watering plants
5, 11, 16, 17
wells 8

Notes for parents and teachers

- Safety outdoors. Explain the dangers of water when children are near the sea, a lake, pond, or river. They should not approach these unaccompanied and should never enter the water. Explain the dangers of drowning and take the opportunity to encourage them to learn to swim.

- Safety at home. Explain the dangers of any volume of water, including baths, ponds, and paddling pools. Children should never leave a faucet running and should understand that problems with water pipes should be dealt with by a plumber.

- It may be difficult for children to appreciate how different the water situation is in developing countries. There are many more facts on the world's water crisis and water stress at www.worldwatercouncil.org*. World Water Day (supported by the United Nations) is on March 22.

- Consumption of bottled water varies around the world. Average annual consumption per person in gallons—Italy 50 gallons (184 liters), France 38 gallons (142 liters), US 24 gallons (91 liters), UK 10 gallons (37 liters), Australia 8 gallons (30 liters) and South Africa 0.5 gallons (2 liters). The world average is 6 gallons (24 liters).

- There are many more fascinating facts about the human body and water. If you weigh 66 pounds (30 kilograms), about 44 pounds (20 kilograms) is made up of water, which is 42 pints (20 liters). Water is an essential part of blood and helps to carry nutrients around the body. We lose water when we breathe out, sweat, and pass urine. We need to replace it by drinking lots of fresh water every day. We might survive without food for more than a month, but we would only survive for a few days without water.

- Look through the book and talk about the pictures. Read the captions and then ask questions about other things in the photographs that have not been mentioned.

Website information is correct at time of going to press. However, the publishers cannot accept liability for any information or links found on third-party websites.